CHRISTMAS GINGERBREAD

STORY AND PICTURES BY JANET WINTER

© THE MEDICI SOCIETY LTD · LONDON 1990   *Printed in England.*   ISBN 0 85503 160 3
Distributed exclusively in the USA by Marian Heath Greeting Cards, Inc., Wareham, Massachusetts.

On Christmas Eve someone left the lid off the biscuit tin.

Three little gingerbread girls
and three little gingerbread boys climbed out.

They played tag all round the kitchen.

They played hide-and-seek in the larder.

They spilt the cat's milk and
they tickled the cat's tail.

The cat was not pleased.
They ran away quickly, across the hall and into the sitting room.

'Oh look,' they shouted, 'look at all these toys and presents.'

They had such fun playing that they woke up Timothy mouse.

'I love Christmas gingerbread,' said the hungry little mouse.

Timothy mouse declared that he did not like gingerbread after all.

'What a mess we have made,' said the gingerbread boys.
'We should pick everything up now,' said the gingerbread girls.

On Christmas morning Mother said,
'Someone's been playing in my kitchen.'

Father said, 'Where is all the gingerbread?'
The children said, 'We'll find it.'

They found one, two, three gingerbread girls.
They found one, two gingerbread boys.

'Where is the last gingerbread boy?' asked Father.
'I can see him!' shouted the littlest child.

'Why that naughty little gingerbread boy,' laughed Mother.
'How did he ever get up there?'